Christmas 1993
or
Santa's Last Ride

An absolutely amazing Christmas story

by
Leslie Bricusse

illustrated by
Errol Le Cain

ff

faber and faber
LONDON · BOSTON

The months, like hens' eggs, come in twelves,
And legend says twelve million elves
All work non-stop the whole year round,
In workshops no one's ever found,
Preparing what is known with pride
As Santa Claus's Christmas Ride.

At least, that's how it used to be,
Till Christmas, 1993,
When something very strange occurred,
Of which, in case you haven't heard,
It's my intent to tell you now.
It caused The All-Time Christmas Row.

Of course, there'd been disputes before –
Like Christmas, 1324,
Which elves today still say had been
The worst dispute they'd ever seen.
They don't discuss it now, because
They've all forgotten what it was.

And then again, in 1510,
There was that famous Christmas when
The Packing Elves ran out of string,
With which they tied up everything.
So one of them invented glue.
That was a sticky Christmas, too.

But back to 1993 –
The job quite clearly is for me
To tell you this amazing tale –
To follow the amazing trail
That Santa blazed that famous year
To bring the world its Christmas cheer.

The Santa saga, may I say,
Is not the tale of just one day.
No, Operation Santa Claus
Takes all year long, without a pause.
But things went badly wrong, you'll see,
That Christmas, 1993.

Our story starts on January One.
A Brand New Year has just begun.
Another Christmas has been kept.
For one full week, the elves have slept,
Recovering from the Yule before,
And gathering strength for one Yule more.

And when they wake, the plans are laid –
The whole year's Christmas programme made.
The zillion things the elves must do
Have been mapped out by You-Know-Who.
Eleven months and three short weeks
Remain to iron out all the creaks.

The world has changed, there is no doubt,
Since Santa's reindeer first set out,
In crystal skies and sparkling snow,
So many thousand moons ago.
And Santa's job back then was fun.
The year, let's not forget, was One.

Life here on Earth was easy then.
To start with, there were fewer men,
With simple thoughts and simple taste,
Who lived their lives in peace, not haste.
Who were content with far, far less,
And liked a thing called Happiness.

So Santa's journey was a breeze.
No problem pleasing folk like these.
No need for an exotic gift
To give their childlike hearts a lift.
How gracefully it all was done
Way back at Christmas Number One.

In those days, there were just twelve elves,
And they did all the work themselves.
They made the toys, prepared the sleigh,
Sent Santa off on Christmas Day –
And Santa managed easily
To be back home in time for tea.

But down the years things slowly changed,
And bit by bit they rearranged
The simple schedule they had once,
Until it took not days but months
To organize their Christmas plan,
And feed the growing needs of man.

No more that simple sleigh-ride now.
The Santa business grew – and how! –
Until by 1644
He couldn't manage any more.
And so a new idea unfurled –
To set up bases round the world.

If all the hungry kids on Earth
Were going to get their Christmas-worth,
It seemed to Santa he would need
Some stopping points, where he could feed
His reindeer, and re-load his sleigh,
Before continuing on his way.

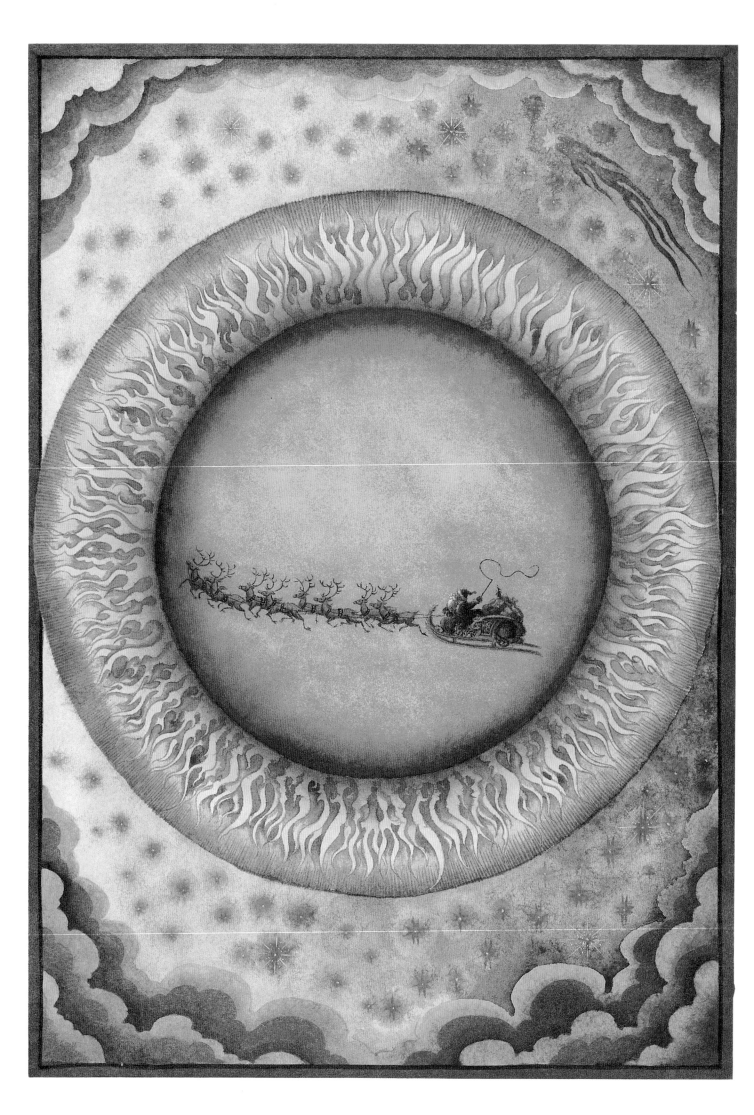

Then Santa tried another ploy,
Which brought a fleeting glimpse of joy.
He found by travelling *with* the sun,
From east to west, the Christmas run
Gained several hours – a clever plan
Much later used by Superman.

But every year the problem grew,
Until, by 1992,
Poor Santa Claus was in despair,
And fit to tear his snowy hair.
He didn't, though extremely galled.
(One hates to think of Santa bald.)

He said, "At age two thousand plus,
I am not one to make a fuss,
But it is time that mankind knew
They've made my work too hard to do."
When things got worse in '93,
He said, "My friends, that's it for me!"

To find out just what Santa meant,
We asked the kindly, wise old gent
To tell us all what galled him so.
And since he felt we ought to know,
He told us of That Fateful Day.
We sat and listened in dismay.

"In olden times," he said with glee,
"When it was just twelve elves and me,
The Christmases were much more fun.
We used to get the wrapping done
In half a day, or maybe less,
And in an hour clean up the mess.

"By eight o'clock on Christmas Eve,
The sleigh was loaded, set to leave.
The twelve elves waved their fond goodbyes,
And high up in the Christmas skies
I waved back down and vowed to be,
As usual, home in time for tea.

"The reindeer sped me through the night –
We must have been a splendid sight –
From north to south, from east to west,
And scarcely stopping for a rest,
The gifts delivered, they had *me*
Delivered, too, in time for tea.

"But nowadays, since men are fools,
And fill the world with stupid rules,
Creating problems they don't need,
And living lives of graft and greed,
They make each Christmas misery
For easy-going folk like me.

"What happens now is quite absurd.
At 6 a.m. on January third
They wake me from my Christmas sleep.
I have so many dates to keep,
If I don't start by January four,
The Christmas plans are on the floor.

"There's half a billion people more
To deal with than the year before,
Plus Customs documents galore,
To make sure I don't break the law
By taking gifts to any land
In ways that might seem underhand.

"I need all sorts of visas, too,
To prove that I'm just passing through.
My passport, numbered North Pole One,
Can end up weighing half a ton.
And even though they know I'm me,
I can't import things duty-free.

"They jab my reindeer with vaccine,
And threaten them with quarantine.
I fill in fifty million forms,
And deal with petty government storms.
United Nations' folk are deaf –
Except the few at UNICEF.

"My team of Lawyer Elves explores
The world, to check on all new wars.
To visit lands like these, you see,
I need to have immunity –
And prove to them as well, of course,
I am not an invading force.

"Now all this stuff, you realize,
Devours my Januarys-to-Julys,
And August and September, too!
The year is now three-quarters through
Before I call the Transport Elf
To organize the Trip itself.

"That's not so bad, I hear you say.
He's made that trip each Christmas Day
Since further back than who-knows-when.
You're right, of course – but way back then
I didn't have to share the sky
With all those airplanes flying by . . .

". . . And satellites and other things –
A lot of which have not got wings.
Now everywhere I need to land,
I have to have air clearance planned.
If I'm delayed by just one plane,
Your Christmas goes straight down the drain."

"These aggravations all combined
Make Christmas something else, I find,
Than what it first was meant to be.
Man has too short a memory,
And thinks of Christmastime, I feel,
As one more chance to cheat and steal.

"Through all of this, twelve million elves
Are stacking gifts on warehouse shelves.
Believe you me, it takes a lot
Of skill to work out who gets what.
To make quite sure no child gets missed,
The Who-Gets-What Elf has this list.

"The Who-Gets-What List's very long –
Some several million pages strong.
A thousand names on every page,
With everyone's address and age.
Old Who-Gets-What's a clever elf –
He writes the whole thing out himself.

"The list weighs sixty-seven tons,
And carries in it everyone's
Ideas on what they'd like to see
Wrapped up beneath their Christmas tree.
The grown-ups' list is quite refined.
The kids' list, though, will blow your mind.

"Oh boy, the things that list contains! –
Forget toy boats and choo-choo trains.
We have an Elf with Outsize Brains
Who studies it and then explains
What Space Wars and Transmutants are.
I sometimes think man's come too far.

"But that is up to man, not me.
It's Santa Claus's job to see
The whole world gets one happy day
Once every year, each in his way.
And that I do, as best I can –
With precious little help from man.

"For if you think my tale so far
Is all there is to tell, you are
Mistaken in the gravest way –
What happened this last Christmas Day,
Which I will tell you now, my friend,
Will make your hair stand straight on end."

So Santa then described to us,
Quite simply, without any fuss,
His Christmas, 1993.
"And when I'm done," he said, said he,
"Then you tell me, for what it's worth,
If there is still goodwill on Earth.

"My take-off time has always been
Just after dinner – nine fifteen.
My sleigh, as usual, looked quite new.
The reindeers' coats were shining, too.
But then I noticed several elves
Were arguing among themselves.

"I asked the Senior Elf-In-Charge,
Who's two foot six and rather large,
What they were arguing about,
And he told me 'There's little doubt
That making toys they do not like
Could one day cause the elves to strike.'

"Now this they'd never done before,
Excepting once, in AD 4.
But that was long enough ago
For nobody to really know
If elves, whom everybody likes,
Enjoy the thought of starting strikes.

"The loyalest creatures ever born,
Elves love to work, and do, till dawn.
They're creatures of tradition, too,
Preferring ancient ways to new.
And modern-day technology
Is therefore not their cup of tea.

"Today you need a science degree
To make toys for a child of three,
Plus all the new computer tricks
To satisfy a child of six.
Most elves can only carve and paint.
And so theirs was a just complaint.

"The older elves have worked for me
Since 1 or 2 or 3 AD.
We've been good friends for all these years,
So naturally I calmed their fears,
And vowed that I would sort things out
Before next Christmas came about.

"The elves embraced and raised a cheer.
(They like to do that every year.)
They fed the reindeer Christmas punch,
To keep them warm till Christmas lunch,
Then off into the night we sped,
Quite unaware what lay ahead.

"You know when things start going wrong,
They tend to go wrong all along?
A small thing here – a big thing there –
Until there's chaos everywhere?
Well, that's the way I felt that night –
I *knew* things just weren't going right.

"The world-wide weather was a mess,
From New South Wales to Inverness –
With rain and snow and sleet and smog,
Electric thunderstorms and fog.
And so, in every major town,
They wisely closed the airports down.

"No help to me, I have to say.
Those airports help me find my way.
And so I circled round and round,
Not knowing what was on the ground,
And every second ticking by
Seemed like an hour in the sky.

"I worried Christmas might run late –
The first time since 1108,
When, leaving Greece one starless night,
And turning left instead of right,
I missed the toe of Italy,
And dumped Rome's presents in the sea.

"But finally the weather cleared.
Things weren't as bad as I had feared.
A happy chance had Santa's sleigh
Directly over Santa Fe,
Stacked neatly in the starry heavens
With lots of Boeing 747s.

"In Customs there was more delay,
While I filled in Form 4XK.
Despite it all we made up time,
Through wind and rain and mud and slime.
I breathed again, that battle won.
My troubles, though, had just begun.

"What followed, known in history
As Christmas, 1993,
Will some day take its hallowed place,
When men discuss the human race,
With Stalingrad and Agincourt –
Among the great fights ever fought.

"It was as though, in some strange way,
I saw in one extraordinary day
A miniature kaleidoscope
Of human lunacy and hope –
A well-matched pair, like man and wife,
Who stick together all through life.

"In Africa, a dreadful drought
Cut all our drinking water out.
In Mexico, it was so hot
Three reindeer fainted on the spot.
In Russia, we were stiff with ice.
In Cuba, we were hijacked twice.

"No place on earth seemed safe to be.
A terrorist threw a bomb at me.
A robber almost slit my throat.
Two children tried to steal my coat.
A souvenir hunter clipped my beard.
'My word', I thought, 'the world is weird!'

"My trip across the USA
Did not exactly make my day.
In Pittsburgh, I was mugged by thugs.
In Boston, stopped for smuggling drugs.
And New York's toys were snatched by thieves.
'Twas not the best of Christmas Eves.

"They asked if I'd go on TV?
And would I vote for GOP?
And would I use this new shampoo?
(They'd pay me lots of money to.)
And trade my sleigh in for a car?
What funny folk Americans are!

"A thousand other things went wrong,
From Nicaragua to Hong Kong.
In Poland, state police challenged me
To prove my own identity.
They then announced I broke six laws
By dressing up as Santa Claus.

"And England, too, was hard to like.
The entire country was on strike.
The London fog so thick and damp,
I couldn't see my driving lamp.
And then we got a parking fine,
Delivering gifts and food and wine.

"In Iceland, they were very rude.
They stopped me for importing food –
Two tons of finest reindeer meat –
Which I explained were *not* to eat!
They tried to buy. I wouldn't sell.
The reindeer thought that just as well.

"One country wouldn't let me in,
Convinced I wasn't genuine.
Another crazy nation said
My politics, like my clothes, were red.
And yet a third gave me the axe
Unless I paid them income tax!

"Three countries changed their names this year,
Plus two I never knew were here.
The two that were not here before
Are now engaged in all-out war.
They'll wipe each other out, and then
Next year they won't be here again!

"In fact, as far as I could tell,
The whole wide world just wasn't well.
Not something I could see, or find,
But more a sickness of the mind.
It had to do with something strange –
Man's never-ending need for change.

"So on and on, around the world,
This trip-to-end-all-trips unfurled.
A thousand stops in half a day,
As Warehouse Elves piled high the sleigh
With endless gifts for everyone,
But somehow it just wasn't fun.

"But since my mission was goodwill,
I struggled on through good and ill.
The ill by far outweighed the good,
As any fool could tell it would.
I stayed in Christmas mood, because
You have to if you're Santa Claus.

"The endless night that leads the way
From Christmas Eve to Christmas Day
Was not, in 1993,
The joyous thing it's meant to be.
I folded up my empty sack,
And felt I'd been to hell and back.

"I felt completely empty, drained.
The reindeer seemed remote, restrained.
They limped across the morning sky,
And Christmas drifted slowly by.
But whether it was foul or fair
I do not know. I do not care.

"My only thought was going home,
And vowing nevermore to roam.
Two thousand years man's seen me here.
I've had a pretty good career.
Perhaps it's time I took a rest.
Perhaps it would be for the best.

"I patted every reindeer's head,
And sent them quietly off to bed.
I thanked my loyal and trusted elves,
Who lay exhausted on the shelves.
And then I sighed and told them, 'Men,
I'll never go through that again.

" 'I never want to take my sleigh
Around a world that lives that way.
I've got no time for people who
Just take for granted what we do.
Things have to change, and if they don't,
When *they* want Christmas, Santa won't!' "

This chronicle of misery
Explains why Christmas, '93,
Will, like Pearl Harbor, always be
A day that lives in infamy –
And proof that Christmas must be freed
From man's stupidity and greed.

And that's the story, sad but true,
That he told me, that I tell you.
It's hard to think of Christmas Day
Without his jingle bells and sleigh.
But Santa's point was loud and clear,
And next year's getting awfully near.

Let's learn from 1993
What Christmas really ought to be,
Or else, by 1994,
There'll be no Christmas any more.
But if we do what we *should* do,
Please God, this story won't be true.

For Evie,
who is always Christmas

The illustrations are for Dean, Alfi, Frederika,
Jean and Alexander with love

First published in 1987 by Faber and Faber Limited
3 Queen Square London WC1N 3AU

Photoset by Parker Typesetting Service Leicester
Printed in Great Britain by
W. S. Cowell Ltd Ipswich

British Library Cataloguing in Publication Data

Bricusse, Leslie
Christmas 1993, or, Santa's last ride
I. Title   II. Le Cain, Errol
821'.914   PZ8.3

ISBN 0-571-14651-1